Metaphorosis

August 2019

Beautifully made speculative fiction

Also from Metaphorosis Books

Score – an SFF symphony

Reading 5X5: Readers' Edition
Reading 5X5: Writers' Edition

Best Vegan Science Fiction & Fantasy

Best Vegan SFF of 2018
Best Vegan SFF of 2017
Best Vegan SFF of 2016

Metaphorosis Magazine

Metaphorosis: Best of 2018
Metaphorosis: Best of 2017
Metaphorosis: Best of 2016

Metaphorosis 2018: The Complete Stories
Metaphorosis 2017: The Complete Stories
Metaphorosis 2016: Nearly Complete Stories

Monthly issues

by B. Morris Allen

Susurrus
Allenthology: Volume I
Tocsin: and other stories
Start with Stones: collected stories
Metaphorosis: a collection of stories

Metaphorosis

August 2019

---

edited by
B. Morris Allen

Metaphorosis Books

Neskowin

ISSN: 2573-136X (online)
ISBN: 978-1-64076-145-2 (e-book)
ISBN: 978-1-64076-146-9 (paperback)

August 2019

Never Fade Away..7
    by Claire Simpson

A Bear, or a Spider, or an Elephant.........37
    by Edward Ashton

The Last Duty...49
    by Dawn Lloyd

The Propagator..73
    by Simone Kern

There is a City, He Told Me...................113
    by Evan James Sheldon

Never Fade Away

Claire Simpson

"Miz Ellerker?"

The old woman looked up from where she was kneeling in her garden, tending to the tiny green shoots that were poking through the soil. "There's a name I ain't heard in a while," she said to the young whippersnapper shifting from foot to foot on the far side of her gate. "I've gone by a few others in the years since then."

"But you are Miz Ellerker?" the kid persisted.

"I was." She pushed a little more soil around a shoot to keep it safe. "Will that do you?"

"I got a message." He thrust a clenched fist with a crumpled paper in it over the gate. "It's urgent."

"Always is by the time they call for me." She shifted a little, then looked the kid up and down. "Come here and give me a hand."

The gate rattled as he pushed it open, betraying the quiver in his arm. "I don't know much about planting."

"But you've got two hands, I can see, and that means you can hold one of them out for me." As he did so she slapped her own left hand, bony and twisted from illness in her youth, into his and used his strength to haul herself to her feet. "There we go." She dusted her knees and assessed the kid again. Barely old enough to be out of doors and yet already taller than her. Not that that was hard, with all the years pushing down on her tired shoulders. "I know what you're thinking. '*This* is our Last Hope? She'll barely make it to the end of the street, let alone save us from our troubles.'"

"I..." The kid was blushing under the dirt and sweat. "I didn't..."

"Just give me the letter and then we'll see what kind of a chance you might have."

She had to smooth out the creases, teasing the paper back to a semblance of flat before she could read the words, but it wasn't like she needed to see them to know what it said. The note said what they always said. *Please come. Please help us. We'll give you what you ask.* After all these years, she was still the Last Hope. The requests were the same; only the places changed.

It had been years since the last one, so long that she'd thought they'd stopped coming. Hoped, maybe, but not so much that she'd stopped making sure she could be found. A discreet advert here, a word or two to the right people there, just enough for the truly desperate to be able to track her down.

"All right then," she sighed. "Just let me fix up a few things. You had to show up in planting season, didn't you?"

"We couldn't wait any longer," he mumbled.

"I ain't blaming you. Just noting that it's always the way of these things." She strolled to the fence that separated her land from her neighbour and hollered until the matron next door emerged. "I got urgent business taking me away for a few days. You mind sending one or two of your youngsters to take care of the planting till I return?"

"Never a problem to have a way of keeping them out of mischief," the matron said with a smile and a wink at the kid. "What's left to do?"

"Mainly just watering to make sure they all come through strong. But there's some potatoes still working on sprouting, and I'd be much obliged if those could be planted when they're ready." She fixed the kid fidgeting at her side with a withering glare. "Don't be thinking this ain't important. If nobody plants my potatoes what'll I eat come the winter? Ain't nobody going to be *my* Last Hope when I'm starving."

"It's urgent," he said again.

"Ain't nothing so urgent I can't set things straight round here first." She nodded to her neighbour and stumped back into the house with the kid trailing behind her.

In deference to the kid's anxiety she didn't spend time straightening all the messes she could see outstanding as she moved around. They could think what they liked about her housekeeping while she was gone. She stuffed things into a bag, nothing but a few essentials for the journey, muttering to herself as she wandered the rooms trying to keep track of it all.

"Do me a favour, kid," she said when she thought she had everything else prepared. "There's a large wooden box under my bed. Haul it on out and put it up where I can reach it." No sense locking her back scrabbling round under there herself when the kid was hopping about with nothing to keep him occupied.

The kid did as she bade him, grunting as he dragged the box across the floorboards and into the daylight. He tried to lift it onto the bed but couldn't get more than one end up in the air.

"All right, kid, don't strain yourself," she said after a minute. "Right there is just fine. Mind out of the way now."

She bustled him aside and flipped the latches on the box with military sharpness. From beneath layers of sentimental keepsakes she withdrew two things; a small pouch that clinked gently as it disappeared into one of her pockets; and a revolver in a thick leather belt. She buckled the belt good and tight before removing the revolver and opening it with practised hands, inspecting the barrel and the chambers before she snapped it back together and dropped it into the holster.

The kid's eyes were wide and he swallowed hard. He opened his mouth, but no sound came out and eventually he just shut it again.

"Be a dear and shove that back under the bed before we leave," she said, nodding toward the box and stumping out of the room. While he was trying to be an unstoppable force, she slipped the pouch from her pocket and checked the contents. Not as much as there used to be, that was for sure, but enough. There were only so many more times she could expect to be called on, after all.

Perhaps it would have been better if she'd stopped advertising after all. She was tired, her bones weighted with weariness, and a quiet retirement in a little cottage with a patch of garden for her vegetables was most of all she could manage. But the call had come, and she'd be damned if she wouldn't answer it just the same as always. That was what it meant, to be a Last Hope.

The kid, panting from his efforts, was ushered out the door and she turned the key in the lock even though she then just tucked the key under a rock on the doorstep. One last look around the garden, checking for anything she might have missed, and they went out of the gate and away down the road.

"Ask your question, kid. You keep opening your mouth like that and you'll end up catching flies."

The kid gaped at her a while longer like she was some kind of mind-reader. At last he found both the words and the courage at the same time. "Where are we going?" he asked, his voice hoarse. "You were supposed to be coming with me to save the town, but this ain't the way. Not the quickest way, anyhow."

"Of course it ain't," she said, chuckling to herself. "What, you think we're just going to stride up Main Street and shoot the bastard that's causing all your grief?"

"That's why you brought the gun, ain't it?" He kicked a stone up the road ahead of him, the slump of his shoulders a mere ghost of the full surliness that would come for him given a year or two more.

"This old thing?" She patted the gun on her hip. "Bless you, this is only for scaring off trouble on the road. I wouldn't waste bullets on your feller. Hell, if you wanted him shot, there were people closer who could have done the job."

"He's got them all scared." His voice dropped so low she had to strain to catch the words. "Put my brother in the dirt just for looking at him funny. Mama just stood and watched, then fixed him his plate like always. Weren't nothing else she could have done without ending in the dirt herself, so she said, and then who'd take care of the rest of us?"

"And you expect me just to walk up to him with my gun out? You think a man who doesn't hesitate to put a kid in the dirt will hold off on an old woman?" She laughed again but there was no humour in it. "You never learned about the Last Hope? Maybe that's for the best, when it's all over and done. But for right now," she left the road, aiming for a boulder with a nice flat top under the shade of a tree, "I need to take the weight off my feet."

"Again?" The kid threw himself down in the dirt as she settled onto the boulder. "We'll never get there at this rate."

"You want to take my gun and see if you can save me the bother of the rest of the walk?" She pulled it from the holster and offered him the handle. "You feel free.

I'll be along in my own time to claim it off your corpse." Ignoring his complaints, she leaned on her knees and waited for her breath to return.

The kid was twitchy, getting to his feet several times to stare impotently up the road or dance around her before flopping back down with an impatient huff. "You remember I told you it was urgent, right?"

She'd closed her eyes, not to sleep but just to rest them, but now her head jerked back up at his words. "I remember." She wiped a thread of drool from her chin. "And I know it must feel that way. Took you folks so long to find the courage to call for me, you're afraid it'll flit away again before I arrive. But I need to know more about what I'll be facing if I'm to do my job. So why don't you pass the time here by telling me this bastard's history?"

"I don't know the whole of it." He seemed to shrink into himself, all that impatience and bravado crumbling away. "I was only a kid when he came. We liked him back then. He was all charm and friendliness, and he made Mama smile for the first time since Pop was killed. He said someone needed to do something about all the trouble in the town, and then he said he could be the one to help us."

"That's how it starts." She stretched out, feeling the joints in her back and shoulders crack, and thought of every charming man with a powerful temper she'd ever crossed paths with, right back to her own father. "You'd never have given him the time of day if he hadn't known how to charm you. That didn't last though, right?"

"I think it was my fault." He whispered it to the dirt in front of him. "I was young and careless. I made him angry. He got so angry with me for stepping out of line, and after that it was like no one could make him happy. Not even Mama."

"If it hadn't been you it would have been someone else." She spat on the ground and started the process of hauling herself to her feet. "Sooner or later someone always makes them angry. And once they think they're being disrespected, they start to see it everywhere."

The kid offered her his hand, pulled her up without even being asked. He was a good kid. "He whupped Billy Preston for laughing too loud as he was walking by. Threw Old Ma Preston in a cell for a night for daring to complain about it. That was when the town really changed, when they figured if he'd do that to an old lady there was no telling what he'd do to the rest of them."

"And still you think I should just walk in there and confront him?" She started along the road again. Now the kid had opened up there'd be plenty of time for him to tell her the rest as they walked.

"He's in there all right." The kid came rushing out of the town in the early morning light, out of breath but somehow bursting with energy despite a poor night spent dozing in a ditch. "I knew he wouldn't leave town, not for nothing."

"Excellent." She got to her feet, joints popping and cracking as she stretched out as straight as she could. "Now I need you to go back in there and keep an eye on him. Make sure he stays within the town limits, okay? Do whatever you have to. Stick to him like glue and don't let him leave, you hear?"

The kid gave a sharp nod and dashed away back into the town. He was a good kid, good enough that she almost felt a pang at what she was asking of him. But the choice wasn't hers; it had been made when he was dispatched with the note begging her to help, and who was she to throw that back in their faces?

One careful step at a time, she measured out the exact centre of the south road into the town, where it always had to start. The ritual demanded an opening approach from the south, though in truth she'd have walked a longer path regardless to get the kid to open up and elaborate on all the ways this bastard was like every other one she'd met. The little details were important; they put the steel in her spine that she'd need if she were to see this through.

When she was certain she had the centre, she looked all around for anyone that might be spying before drawing the pouch out from her pocket. Something small, no bigger than a penny, came out pinched between her finger and thumb and she dropped it onto the ground and covered it over with dirt, stamping down hard until it was hidden.

The pouch went back into her pocket and she stood for a moment, her eyes closed, checking that everything was right. She rested in perfect stillness, grabbing what peace she could before she had to face the storm that was brewing.

She allowed herself a moment, but no more, then she nodded in satisfaction and walked away from the town like she'd never planned to go in there.

She was trying not to admit to herself how tired she was when she approached the town from the west. It was only the second way she had to come, and with the sun determined to keep rising higher in the sky there was no time to rest. Everything had to be ready and waiting while the light was still good or they'd have to waste a whole day waiting and risk everything being undone.

There had been a time when she'd have skipped round the whole town and been done in the time it had taken her to plant just one seed and move on. But there had been times when she'd have done all kinds of things, and none of those times were now. Right now, she just had to do the best she could.

Again she found the centre of the road. There was a little more activity in the town now, so she kept the pouch hidden in her pocket and only drew out the seed, so small as to hardly be noticed. Folks had too many worries to pay much heed to an old woman bending down in the road, but when she straightened back up she caught the eye of a man old by most standards but still young by hers, who nodded in acknowledgement and put a finger to his lips.

She stamped this one into the dirt and now when she closed her eyes she could feel both of them humming to each other. It was faint, of course, because there was only half a pattern but at least she could hear the harmony that said her alignment was close enough. She listened a little longer than she needed to, stealing a moment to catch her breath before turning her back on the town once more.

It would have been quicker to go through the town, but she couldn't enter until all the seeds were planted. There were rules to be followed, and risks to be avoided, and staying outside counted as doing both. The net had to be ready to cast before he had an inkling she was there, otherwise he'd find a way to slip free of it and the town's Last Hope would be wasted.

A long walk, to come at the town again from the north. A stick to lean on, that would have been nice. She'd not thought to get one, not when all she did was work in her garden and take the short walk to buy things from the store twice a week. Funny how the time could creep up on you, make you realise all your age at once.

The sun was high when the third seed was safely planted, but now she knew she could still make it in time. Just one more to go, and she'd be weary when it was done, but that was just fine. She'd have enough strength for what needed to be done, and once it was done nothing more would matter.

Three seeds hummed loud enough to hear even when she wasn't listening for them. The north and the south were well-aligned, linked and sharing what they needed in a strong bond. The west was still a little weaker, but its pair was coming. She promised it that as she hobbled away from the town again.

There was a commotion somewhere in the town as she approached it from the east. A great hollering and banging and a high, keening wail that sounded like it might have been the kid. She couldn't be sure, and even if she could, there was nothing to be done. The fourth seed had to be planted before she entered the town, trouble or no trouble. She just wished the noise hadn't been such a distraction. It was keeping her from hearing the west properly.

Not that she needed to hear it, not after so many years. She found the centre of the road, just like she'd done with the others. She could plant this seed by measurement, without the lazy get-out of listening to the hum. Measurement, and feel, and the knowledge of where it should be even as the wailing grew more desperate.

The seed went in and it was done. After a moment the hum grew until it blocked out everything else unless she worked to ignore it. The links were right and true; west to east; south to north; and all around the outside. The circle was complete, and the Last Hope would come.

She pulled the gun from its holster and cradled its comforting weight as she marched up the east road into the centre of the town. It was the kid wailing, she saw when she reached the main square. He was there, on the ground, bloodied and crying as a giant of a man stood over him and kicked and kicked and kicked.

"What would you be doing a thing like that for?" she asked, her voice clear and strong so he had no choice but to stop and look at her.

"This doesn't concern you, grandma," he said, delivering another kick to the kid's ribs. "This is a matter of discipline, and round here that's my job." The sun, on its way down, shone on the metal of his sheriff's badge. It left deep shadows in the lines on his face as he visibly tamped down his anger and turned up the charm. My, but he was a handsome one when he wanted to be. "The boy was disrespectful, so I'm teaching him that misbehaviour has consequences. It'll help him grow into a fine man some day."

The kid looked at her with bloodshot eyes. "I'm sorry," he said. "You told me to keep him here. I couldn't think of anything else to do."

She walked closer, though she was half the size of the sheriff. "This is discipline?" she asked him. "Seems a lot like violence to me. How do you tell the difference?"

"The difference is I'm doing it." He held her gaze and pointed to his badge. "Folks around here made it my job to enforce proper standards of behaviour."

There had been a time when his smile and his easy confidence would have convinced her to drop the matter. But that was long ago, back before she'd met any number of men just like him. Men who were so nice you couldn't believe they'd ever hurt a fly, but their wives always seemed to be sporting poorly-covered bruises. Who were sweetly persuasive until you gave the slightest sign that you disagreed, and then the rage came flaring out. "What if they don't like the way you're doing your job?"

And there it was, though he tried to hide it. The tiniest little twitch in his demeanour at the idea of such defiance. "If anyone has any complaints they can bring them to me. My door is always open."

Closer again, close enough to smell the blood and piss rising from the kid. "He's had enough and you need to stop." The gun was right there in her hand but she didn't raise it.

"You think you can just walk into town and start throwing your weight around?" He was still smiling but his eyes were cold. "You think that little thing gives you the right?" He snatched the gun from her unresisting fingers, snapping it open and scattering the bullets over the kid. "Old woman like you needs to stop giving her nursemaid the slip. It'll get you into trouble, especially around here."

There was a crowd forming around them, people creeping out of their houses and shops to see the show. All keeping their distance, of course, but she could see the desperate words of their letter written across all of their faces. *Please help us. Be our Last Hope. We've been looking the other way so long we don't know anything else.*

"Ain't the gun that gives me authority." She squared up to him, looking up at his flint hard eyes, the kid on the ground between them. "I don't believe we've been introduced. They call me Miz Ellerker." She held out a hand, brittle and gnarled.

He knocked her hand aside and spat on the ground at her feet. "A Fade witch?" he snarled, glaring around at the crowds. "You dared to set a soul sucker on me?" The flip from charm to rage was so sudden she would have flinched if she hadn't been expecting it.

The crowd gave no answer, unless you counted the mass shuffling of feet and staring at the ground.

"You'll come to regret it," he told them. "I'll see to that, don't you worry, just as soon as I've dealt with her."

"You're mighty confident," she said, pulling herself a little straighter despite the protests from her bones.

"The Fade works on fear. Everyone knows that, if they know anything about it." He was looming over her, his breath hot on her face. "I ain't afraid of you, old woman."

"Time will tell," she said, not breaking her gaze. "But who said it had to be you that was afraid? There's plenty of fear here for me to use. You made sure of that." She smiled at the flicker of uncertainty in his eyes, and she started to hum.

It was a call, and a response, an acknowledgement and a summoning. She met the hum of the seeds around the town and she pulled them towards her, urging them out of the ground.

The seeds sprouted, bursting up through the dirt and pushing toward the sky. Branches spread, roots dug deep, until the dark trees overshadowed the town. The links between them thickened, becoming tangible, the air turning oily. The lines met exactly in the centre of the town square, right where she stood, and as she called and they pulled, she dragged the sheriff with her into the Fade.

"Miz Ellerker?" The kid was laying on his back staring up at the void where the sky used to be.

"Stay down, kid," she said. "Close your eyes and wait for this to be over." He did as he was told. He was a good kid. They were always good kids. Just once she'd have liked an incorrigible rascal, just to see if that made it any easier.

The sheriff had staggered as she pulled him in, but he recovered quickly. "Bitch," he spat. "You think you can beat me, even in here? I'll deal with you and then I'll make every last one of them pay for trying it. Starting with this one." He went to kick the kid again, but the roots of the dark trees were spreading and they caught his feet. "What in hell?"

Her own feet were bound and the kid was vanishing beneath the tangle of roots. She stood calm, humming a note of welcome. "It ain't your job to administer discipline in here."

"I'm going to enjoy killing you," he said as the kid whimpered inside his cage of roots. "It'll be slow and painful, I promise you." The Fade thickened around him, tendrils of dark shadow reaching toward her.

"You think I'm scared of death?" She waved her hand and the shadows blew away on the breeze. "Maybe once, I'll grant you, when I was young and new to this. But now? Now I stand and talk with her every morning, and I know it'll be no bad thing when she comes for me. Hell, at least that way I'll get some peace and quiet."

She bent, wincing at how quickly she was stiffening. The roots slackened as she stroked them and she eased her feet out. The sheriff tried to copy her, but for him they only tightened.

"Here's the thing," she said, stepping around the kid to move up close to the sheriff. "You weren't wrong when you said the Fade needs fear. It's built on it. It craves it. I planted the seeds but the dark trees could never have grown if the town weren't overflowing with fear. And the big secret, the one you were hoping I didn't know?" She stretched up to whisper in his ear. "You're the most scared of all of them."

He lashed out at her then, the back of his fist slamming into her chest. She didn't fall because the Fade held her up, thickening into a cushion behind her, but something inside cracked, a line of fire through her sternum.

"See?" she coughed, hunching over the hurt. "Got you so scared you had to hit an old woman."

"You're no woman," he snarled. "You're a soul sucker."

"I'm the Last Hope for this town," she said. "You got them all so damn scared they can't do a damn thing to stand in your way but beg for the Fade. And the Fade always comes when it's called."

She winced again as she lowered herself to sit on the ground by the kid. He was entirely covered by roots now. They came nosing around her, but she brushed them aside. "Brave of the kid to try to stop you leaving. I knew I could count on him," she said, patting the cage that was now thick enough to muffle the cries from inside. "But brave ain't about not being scared. He was scared when he stood up to you, and terrified when you started beating him. Almost as scared as you were to think folks might stop doing what you tell them. You've been lashing out for years, terrified that if you didn't no one would ever pay you any mind and you'd die of insignificance."

Every breath burned inside her, but she had to stay calm. The Fade wouldn't take her, not after all these years. She wouldn't let it have any claim on her.

"Did you think it would be different when you first came here? When you came riding in as the big damn hero, did you think this was it? This was the time you'd finally get the respect you deserved?"

"These small-town assholes are all the same." He spat on the ground at her feet. "Never do appreciate all the good I do for them. I try being nice, but sooner or later they all spit in my face. I cracked down harder here, tried to instil some real discipline, and what did it get me? They'd rather call the Fade than tip their hat to me in the street."

"Seems to me you're getting every scrap of respect that you deserve. When everyone you meet strikes you as an asshole? That's the time to consider that the problem is with you."

The roots were climbing up the sheriff's legs and over his knees already. The more they climbed, the angrier he got, but that only encouraged them. If he'd been willing to concede a need for change, maybe it might have been different.

"Please," he said, remembering his manners only when the plants covered his shoulders. "Please. Give me a chance."

"The time for that is long gone," she said conversationally. "You already had your chances, and you didn't bother with any of them until your back was against the wall. By this point I'm just sticking around to see they finish the job properly."

And with that she just sat, humming to herself with shallow breaths, until the roots climbed over the sheriff's head. The last word she heard from him was a curse.

"I'm sorry," she said to the kid, though he couldn't have heard her.

The town was overshadowed by the dark trees that grew on every side. In a few generations it would be swallowed by the forest, but for now folks were free. In the centre of the square the shadows of the sheriff and the kid lingered, ghostly and unsettling. The crowds had dispersed, but they would never be allowed to forget what they'd done here.

She stood in the square, one hand clutched to her chest where the fire was growing now she was out of the Fade. It was going to be a long walk home.

Another woman was there, crouched in the dirt, weeping over the shadow of the kid. "I hoped it wouldn't be true," she said. "I hoped you wouldn't take him."

"But you sent him anyway. You gave your kid to the monster so he might pass you by. And not for the first time, either. He told me what you let happen to his brother. Was this one easier or harder to choose?"

The mother rounded on her, eyes blazing with fury, but halfway up something snapped inside her and she slumped back down. "Both were far too easy," she whispered. "It was them or me, and I didn't hesitate. Who would make such a choice?" She reached for her child, but her hand went straight through.

"Seems to me you ain't had many choices worth making in some time." She placed a hand on the mother's back. "That ain't forgiveness, but it's understanding, and that's better than nothing."

It really was a shame about the kid. He'd been a good boy, from all she'd seen. But she'd needed his fear to make the dark trees grow, and there was no coming back from that. They'd been mighty clear that the job needed to be done.

"Just because you made a choice, doesn't mean you wanted what you chose," she said to no one in particular. "Just means the alternative was worse. Maybe I'd never have chosen to learn the tricks of the Fade, if my other option weren't starving to death on the street." She sighed. "Never took anyone on myself for the learning, but maybe I just never found anyone desperate enough that I'd give them that choice." She cast an eye over at the trees. They'd see to it that she remembered she what she'd done here, what she'd chosen to do. Just like all the other times that still lingered with her at night.

"Here's your payment." The man who'd acknowledged her earlier was at her shoulder, holding out a purse. "Everything as agreed." He wouldn't make eye contact with her now, and as soon as she took the money, he nodded and turned away.

The town would die, slowly. The trees would stand forever as a testament to what the folks there had done, and the dark dreams they brought would discourage folks from lingering. But it would die on its own terms now, and maybe some few would escape to better lives. It wasn't for her to judge. It was her job only to be the Last Hope when they asked her to, knowing the consequences.

With a stout branch claimed from one of the dark trees as a support, she turned her back on the town and headed for home. There were seedlings to take care of, and maybe still some potatoes left to plant.

See Claire Simpson's story "Never Fade Away" online at Metaphorosis.
If you liked it, leave a comment. Authors love that!
Remember to subscribe to our e-mail updates so you'll know when new stories are posted.

About the story

The whole of this story grew from the opening scene, which is unusual for me. Usually when I write I have some concept of the plot, or at least the ending, but here I had nothing more than the image of the old woman working in her garden and the kid showing up to drag her out of retirement.

The rest of the story was essentially a dialogue between the two characters; the kid expected a gun-toting hero so of course there was a revolver in a box under the bed; the old woman said any fool could fire a gun, and there had to be another reason why they needed her specifically, and that's when the pouch of seeds appeared. And so it went on, right the way to the end when she told me what was going to happen to the kid.

When the first draft was complete, I was lucky enough to have a beta reader pick up on what became the main theme of the story: the choices we make when there are no 'good' options beyond survival. There are no heroes in this world, only people trying to make it through another day. The later drafts were worked with this in mind, along with the knowledge of how the story would end. It really is a shame; he was a good kid.

A question for the author

Q: How often do you think about writing during a day?

A: I think about writing in inverse proportion to my ability to write at any given moment. When I'm at work, I'm forever musing on story ideas and wishing I could be writing. When I have free time, suddenly there are a thousand and one other things to think about, all of them more interesting. I try, as far as possible, to nurture the ideas when they come, often making notes on my phone, because knowing what I'm going to write vastly increases the chances that I'll actually write it.

About the author

Claire Simpson writes code by day and stories by night (or at least that's what she claims to be doing when she's actually looking at Twitter). Congenitally incapable of doing nothing, she also sews, crochets, and favours a peaty single malt if you're buying.

@RexMagenta

A Bear, or a Spider, or an Elephant

Edward Ashton

"The night sky is beautiful," Seven says. "Deep and dark, blue-black and starless. It has a certain ineffable purity to it, don't you think?"

Mara glances up. This world is a young one, snugged tight against the galactic core. The stars above her are so fat and bright and crowded together that this can barely be called a proper night at all. She looks back to Seven, one eyebrow raised.

"Not here," he says, his face twisting into a delicate scowl. He's human tonight, mostly, though it seems to Mara that he's gotten some of the proportions wrong.

"This night sky is a trollop. I was speaking of home."

Something cries out in the starlit half-dark in a voice like a child's. Seven seems not to notice, but Mara feels a cold shiver run the length of her spine. She leans over to pick a handful of thin branches from the pile she's assembled, snaps the longer ones in half, then drops them onto the fire.

"I envy you," she says. "I barely remember my home."

Seven shrugs, with a rippling motion that betrays an extra joint somewhere in his shoulders.

"Mine was lost long before I found you, but I still recall it in great detail."

The soft breeze dies, and the forest falls silent.

"Found me?" Mara says. Her voice is low and even, but her eyes have narrowed to slits. Seven flinches as if he'd been struck.

"A poor choice of words," he says.

"Was it?"

"The night sky..." Seven begins, but Mara cuts him off with a look.

"To say you *found* something," Mara says, "is to imply that it was lost."

Seven sighs, and seems to shrink into himself.

"I was not lost," Mara says.

"No," Seven says. "You were not lost."

"I was not," Mara says, "not until you *found* me."

"*Found* is the wrong word," Seven says. "I concede it. What word should I use?"

Mara leans forward. The fire casts a monstrous shadow behind her.

"A fine question," she says. "I think *abducted* has a nice ring to it."

She waits for Seven to reply, but he has no answer to this. He never does. This conversation, like all their conversations, is a minor variation on a well-worn theme.

In a literal sense, Mara's accusation is unfair. She did, after all, consent to this. She can't help but feel, though, that consent means little without understanding—and when she consented, she had no hope of understanding *forever*.

To Seven, of course, this is incomprehensible. *Forever* is the water he swims through.

Mara turns away, leans back against her pack and closes her eyes. They're in a clearing of sorts, though this world is covered in great woody ferns rather than honest trees. She should probably set a tent. The ground is soft, though, and the fire is warm. She takes a deep breath in, holds it, then lets it out in a long, slow sigh.

"There is no reason to be sad," Seven says.

"There are infinite reasons to be sad," Mara says. "You should know that better than anyone."

"Untrue," Seven says. "There are tragedies, admittedly, and injustices aplenty. The good are swept under, and the evil prosper. In the end, though, the night sky is beautiful."

"But not this one."

"No," Seven says. "Not this one."

Off in the distance, a creature howls. The sound this time is almost familiar. It could be a wolf, Mara thinks—but no, wolves are far from here, on the opposite side of an unbridgeable gulf in both distance and time. The animals on this planet are built to a different body plan— asymmetric, many-legged, and scaly. She's seen them in the distance, moving sinuously through the ferns, covered in mouths and studded with eyes.

Wolves? No.

But still, they might serve.

Once, on a different world, under a different sky, Mara found the courage to ask Seven if he would ever permit her to die.

"Of course," he said. "Everything dies. You, in fact, will be eaten—by a bear, I believe."

Later, he said, "Well, not a bear, exactly. More like a spider, perhaps? Or an elephant? I'm not entirely clear on the distinctions."

Mara smiled.

"Will you ever die, Seven?"

He stared at her until her smile faltered, then shook his head.

"Nothing is eternal, Mara."

Mara wakes in the early hours. The fire has died, and the glare of the starlight at first tricks her into thinking it must be morning. Seven is curled into a ball on the far side of their little campsite, snoring delicately. She sits up. The forest is laid out around her in sharp-bordered patterns of silver and black. Mara climbs silently to her feet. Seven shifts in his sleep, then tucks his head under one arm like a gangly, featherless bird. Mara turns her back to him, and sets off into the ferns.

In the strictest sense of the term, Mara is free, and always has been. She has walked away from Seven before, sometimes for months, and once for what would have been most of a lifetime if she and Seven had never met. Seven never came for her, and when she finally returned, it was as if she'd never left at all.

For Seven, it may actually have felt that way. His relationship with time is a slippery one, and it has sometimes seemed to Mara that to him, the birth and death of the universe are simply the soft, possibly permeable edges of the space he inhabits. Mara, though, is trapped in linear time, and the thread that stretches from this moment to the one where she and Seven first met is exceedingly long. Her memories of home are fragments, frozen bits of flotsam that have somehow managed to lodge in her brain when the narratives surrounding them have long since washed away. One of those comes to her now—a warmth in her palm, the imprint of a tiny hand clinging to hers. Her eyes fill momentarily. She has to stop walking to wipe them clear.

When she looks up, she finds a dozen eyes looking back at her.

"Well," she whispers. "What have we here?"

The tip of a claw brushes the soft skin below her left eye, trails down along her cheek, then traces the line of her jaw. The creature's movements are silent, but Mara feels the passage of air as its body surrounds her. Cold lips kiss her hand, then her throat. Where they touch, numbness spreads. Her knees buckle. A hundred arms are there to catch her. Teeth nip at the back of her thigh, and she feels a brief stab of pain before that too goes numb. The creature is coiled tight around her now, tight enough that her breath comes short and a rising roar fills her ears. Its mouth covers her own, barbed tongue probing. It...

Stops.

"Mara."

She tries to open her eyes, but she's frozen, pinioned in time, trapped along with the creature, along with the forest, along with...

Everything.

"Mara. This creature is not a bear."

No, she thinks. *It is not a bear.*

"This is not a spider, or an elephant."

No, it is not.

"You mustn't die today."

Seven.

Please.

I'm tired.

"Then rest. We can stay on this world for a while."

You're a god, Seven. Just make yourself a new companion.

Seven hesitates then.

Mara can't recall him ever hesitating before.

"I am not a god, Mara."

Really? What are you then?

"I am..."

Again, the hesitation.

"...alone, if you leave me."

Mara sighs.

I am not made for eternity, Seven.

"There is no eternity, Mara. Patience. In the fullness of time, who can say? There may be a bear."

If she could, she would smile.

Or a spider?

"Yes, or a spider. Or perhaps an elephant?"

Mara holds her silence, but she knows now what her answer will be.

"Mara?"

Promise me, Seven.

"I..."

Seven.

"I promise."

The universe *shifts...*

...and Mara is back again at their little campsite, staring into the coals of their long-dead fire. Seven sits across from her, a hopeful smile on his face.

Off in the distance, the many-eyed creatures howl.

See Edward Ashton's story "A Bear, or a Spider, or an Elephant" online at Metaphorosis. If you liked it, leave a comment. Authors love that!

Remember to subscribe to our e-mail updates so you'll know when new stories are posted.

About the story

Most of my shorter pieces start with an image that gets stuck in my head, and won't go away until I figure out something to say about it. In the case of "A Bear, or a Spider, or an Elephant," that image was a night sky, clear and cold, deep black and packed tight with stars.

I do a lot of backpacking, and I've spent many nights alone on peaks and ridges and overlooks, staring up into the night sky and wondering what it might look like from another vantage—far out on the galactic rim, for example, or pressed tight against the core. I've also spent plenty of time on those nights nervously wondering what exactly made that cougar-ish noise I just heard off in the distance. Put those thoughts together, and you've pretty much got the opening scene for this story.

I've often felt that writing a short story is simply a matter of finding an opening image and a closing image, and then figuring out what exactly brings the two together. In the case of this story, that thing was the idea of mortality, and how that relates to freedom. Once I had that, the rest was just a matter of filling in the details.

A question for the author

Q: What hero (of any gender) would you name your child after, if we lived in a society with names like that?

A: Honestly, I don't much believe in heroes. I've never been a fan of the Chosen One trope, and the protagonists in my stories are mostly ordinary people who are forced by circumstance to do extraordinary things despite being manifestly unqualified for the job. That said, I've always had a soft spot for Jonah from Cat's Cradle. If I had a son, maybe I'd go with that?

About the author

Edward Ashton lives in Rochester, New York with his inordinately patient wife, an adorably mopey dog, and a steadily diminishing number of daughters. He studies new cancer therapies by day, and spends his evenings writing speculative fiction, and occasionally trying to explain how an MRI works to an extremely bored sixteen year old girl.

edwardashton.com, @edashtonwriting

The Last Duty

Dawn Lloyd

The fireworks rocketed past the jagged remnants of the palace's roof, soared above the razor wire, and then cascaded down behind the wall. The gunpowder boomed. The first four nights, my eyes had jerked to the remnants of the roof still clinging to charred rafters. I was sure the concussion would shake the last pieces lose, crushing me. But I had not been so lucky, and tonight I closed my eyes to shut out the lights.

Huddled in the corner, Petrov shifted. I opened my eyes to see him struggling to pull the wool blanket tight against the snow. Only two weeks before, the gold-rimmed dome of the palace's great hall had cast a yellow tinge on the empire's largest silk carpet. Now we sat on rubble and slush. The rebels who thought they could rule better than him had looted the gold.

"Are you awake, Jerov?" He asked.

"How could I not be?" I tried to keep the edge out of my voice. I had nothing but the highest regard for the man who had crushed the Charter Rebellion and held the islands together through the bread riots. I closed my eyes yet again, this time against the images of waves crashing over the torn and broken bodies our soldiers had hurled from the cliffs. The images grew still stronger with my eyes closed. There were reasons I was glad I had been Minister of the Finance and not a general.

"I was just thinking," he went on, his voice quiet and shaky, "that the map to the caves where the desalination plant designs are kept surely burned with the rest of my office."

"I have no doubt it did," I assured him.

"You were always better at maps than me," he continued. "Do you think you could sketch it?"

The last sketches I'd seen had been shoved in our face yesterday. The tall palace guard who usually whistled "The Mourners' Revenge" laughed when he waved the cartoons of the rest of the royal family at us. Petrov's wife, my sister, had been stripped naked, the artist exaggerating her breasts and lips absurdly. The first drawing showed her standing by the stocks. The second, with her innards strewn across the barren ground. The last, a flock of vultures vomiting after eating them. The guard had assured us the first two were true, and the last would have been if the rioters had left anything for the birds.

It was my fault. The rioting had increased when we lengthened the period of compulsory military service. Apparently we were supposed to somehow protect the islands without an army. We'd executed over two hundred of the rioters, plus their families, but it hadn't stopped them. The rioting advanced until we heard them at the palace gates, and then the palace itself. Petrov had handed me his own knife and begged me to see to his family if it became necessary. Then he bolted out the door to command the guards, but the quaver in his voice made his intent clear.

I had raced up the steps to where my sister clutched the curtain overlooking the courtyard. I was no fool, nor was I naïve to the mob's intent, but when she turned to me, her eyes begging protection, my hand froze. How could I slice her neck and watch the blood spurt like a common soldier's?

Thankfully, Petrov's voice pulled me from the memory. "The map, Jerov. Could you reconstruct it?"

I snorted. "You think they'd let us buy our lives with that?"

"Don't call me a fool." His voice was soft, quiet. I hadn't called him a fool. I'd only thought it. "We're the only ones who knew about the map, and they won't be able to build any more desalination plants without the designs in the caves. When we die, the plants go with us."

"Right," I muttered, relishing our last revenge.

The night sky flashed blue and green for a moment, tainting the snow the same color. The boom came instants later.

He took a slow, ragged breath. It sounded hollow against the explosions and the cheers. "The aquifers will run dry in less than twenty years. They'll need to be able to build more plants, and without knowing where the caves are, they won't know how to design them."

"If they didn't kill us, we could keep producing water for them. Murdering swine." It had been my own great grandfather who had sponsored the inventor and then suggested we maintain a monopoly on the plants for just this day. Why should the people have them if we were dead?

His dark outline turned to face me. He pulled his legs up, and the blanket around them. "They'll never find that cave on their own."

The blanket slipped from my own shoulders. Cold air slashed across my arms, but seconds passed before I noticed. "You can't be serious. Not now. Not after all this."

"This isn't the people. The people wouldn't turn against me. It's heretics provoking them."

I didn't know how to respond. Was it a greater cruelty to remind him of the crowd chanting for our deaths, or to let him go on with his delusions?

"Heretics that your own people wouldn't even fight. And it wasn't the heretics who did this." I waved at the

blackened   beams   and   razor   wire
shadowing the sky.

Silence settled around us. Through the
clouds, the hazy circles of the two moons
stared down, cold and indifferent.

"Jerov," he said at last, "you didn't
carry out my last request. Do this, at
least, for me."

If I were not so weak, I would have had
my hands at his throat no matter his
station. "Don't," I growled, "don't even
start with that."

"Because it's true?"

"Because," I snapped, but stopped.

He didn't press. A cough penetrated the
darkness, and for a moment I thought he
was crying again, trying to choke down
the sound and hide it. But a flash of red
lit his face and flickered to yellow. His lips
were drawn in a tight line, his face hard.

There was no purpose in arguing with
that expression. I took a deep breath,
staring up at the gray sky as if it would
release me from the truth. I owed him
whatever I could repay, not just because
of his station, but for my sister. Why did
helping our murderers have to be his last
request? Nevertheless, the longer I
thought of protests, the more map lines
and ridges squiggled into my head.

"They'll never believe it even if I do draw a new map."

"They will if we make it look like we were trying to hide it."

"Of course," I let the sarcasm drip from my voice. "Fine. I'm sure the guards will be happy to give us the paper." I went to the door and called, "Hello?"

From down the corridor, close to where his forefathers' portraits hung, where his should have been placed at his death, came drunken laughter.

"Hello!" I shouted again, louder.

"What d'ya want?" a voice slurred back.

What could I say? That we wanted to help them, truly. Their impudent revolt, the murders, the destruction, were all trivial. We still wanted to be the good and caring rulers that we always had been and to protect them from themselves.

"I need help," I tried.

Hoots pierced the darkness until a blue shower and another explosion drowned them out. I turned back to Petrov, triumphant.

He still faced the place I had been sitting. "We're next to the library. You could climb out and get paper from there."

I sighed and retraced my steps.

I spent the next 30 minutes rolling and stacking stones against the wall. My head fell to my hands when I finished, and he spoke.

"I'm sorry. I know you don't think they deserve it."

"I feel our last night would be better spent in prayers." Or better spent in anything.

"When Naimat was a baby, and he fell and cut himself, and then hit the nurse because he didn't want her to put ointment on it, did you abandon him to let the wound become infected?"

"That's different."

"How?"

"They aren't children."

"Of course they are. If they didn't think like children, they wouldn't have tried to overthrow us."

"Tried?" The word stuck in my throat.

He didn't answer, just pointed at the top of the wall meaningfully.

I braced one hand against the wall and began climbing, placing as little weight on any single stone as possible. At the top, straining, I could just reach a handhold where the wall had cracked, but I wasn't strong enough to pull myself up.

He lurched towards me on his good leg. I wanted to tell him to stop. My job was to serve him, not for him to help me. But the truth was, there was nothing more I could do without help.

He reached the pile and braced a shoulder against the wall, making a step for me with his back.

I couldn't.

He took a breath. "Go on. I can't stay here forever."

And so I went, forcing my foot to touch his shoulder and then searching the rocks until at last something jutted up beneath my palm. It was a carved leaf of the grape vine that had latticed the ceiling. I cleared the snow off it and leaned my weight back, testing it in the way I had when, as boys, we had dared each other to climb the lighthouse overlooking the Duralaman Cliffs.

The broken rocks tore at my clothes and skin as I pulled myself up, but I didn't feel it until I panted from the top and looked down the hall. The guards leaned against the table, boots propped against the remnants of portraits clinging to the wall. The nearest one sat with his back to me, waving a crystal and gold goblet in broad, drunken circles as he spoke.

Petrov waved me down, and I realized I was just as visible to them as they were to me. I swung my legs over, found the emptiest place on the floor, and jumped, tumbling forward onto my hand.

Bookcases had fallen, crushing centuries of books beneath them. Others lay scattered on the floor, fragile spines torn. I picked my way through, resisting the urge to straighten and restack the books. Petrov had always scoffed at my love of them.

I was creeping towards the scroll room, having decided they would be the best for a map, when the door opened near my destination and torchlight quavered. I crouched behind a bookcase, lying low to the ground. A pile of books slid under my hand. I grabbed for them, but they slipped anyway. I froze, hoping he would think it was only the weight of the books against each other.

The torch raised higher, moving from side to side, but it came no closer. I realized I had stopped breathing, then wondered why. Was I afraid he would kill me?

Minutes passed before the wooden legs of a chair scraped against tile and the jaunty notes of "The Mourners' Revenge" lilted out to me. He must have sat down by the door.

I had no other choice. I couldn't lie there behind the bookshelf all night, and so carefully I crawled backwards, arms bent, belly barely above the ground, like an alligator reconsidering its route. Wending my way around sprawling piles of books and broken bookcases, at last I reached the far wall and sat up. The guard sat less than ten paces from the scroll room. If I had continued walking my current route, I would have had to pass directly in front of him. Now I needed to squeeze down the corridor by the wall and then dart into the room when he wasn't looking.

The bookcase sheltering me from his vision lay tipped against the wall, allowing me to stand with my head ducked. I crept forward, hand stretched out to guard against the darkness, until at last I reached the end. The door to the scroll room stood four steps away. If he looked away, it would take less than a second to bolt in. If he looked away.

Seconds and then minutes ticked by. My legs began to ache from the tension. If I had something small, I could throw it to distract him, but the books scattering the floor were too big. I had nearly despaired and given in to the idea of sprinting in front of him when a gust of wind from the empty roof made the torch flicker. He looked up at it, and in that moment, I leapt. My feet seemed to pound the ground as I careened around books to hide my footsteps from him. If he heard through his drunkenness, he did not come to investigate.

Once my heart slowed, I reached for the first scroll I saw. The desk back in the corner stood surprisingly well intact, and I took a pen from the corner and a still-intact bottle of ink from the top drawer.

Hiding in the shadow of the door, I waited for perhaps half an hour, wishing I could simply draw the map there. It was too dangerous to wait there long enough for the ink to dry before carrying it back, though, so I watched for an opportunity to repeat my dash to the shelter of the bookcase. At last, his torch burned low and he stood, stretched, and disappeared back through the door.

The return trip was easy. All I had to do was make myself force one foot after the other down onto the books. The bookcases made an easy staircase up the wall. I tucked the scroll under my arm, and deposited the ink and pen in my pocket. What did stains matter now?

From the rock pile, Petrov watched me. I mimed tossing him the scroll, then did so. He caught it with the same deftness he had shown even when we fenced in our youth, and I lowered myself to his side, testing my weight on the rocks that shifted and rolled as I dropped onto them.

At last I sat, resting in front of him.

"You were gone a long time. Did you have problems?" he asked, as if I might have stayed there for the joy of it. Of course, under other circumstances, that might have been true.

"A guard, the one who whistles all the time, came to look. I had to dodge him."

Petrov grunted. "I suppose it wouldn't have mattered if he'd seen you."

"Except I wouldn't have anything to draw on." I stopped, for the first time wishing I had let the guard drag me back.

He just grunted again, opening the scroll and squinting against the shadows to see it. "Which one is it?"

I shook my head. "No idea. It came from the science wall."

"You can draw the map after sunrise? Before the guards come?"

"I should be able to." I shrugged. "But you still haven't told me how you're going to get them to believe it."

He was silent for a time, then. "We could tell a guard to leave it in some unique place. Let him think we expect someone to come. He'd try to sell it instead."

"Tell?" I corrected.

"Yes." Then, softer as the realization sunk. "Yes, I see your point." He paused and my mind worked against the problem when he went on. "A bribe, perhaps?"

Etiquette and years of respect kept me from snorting. "Bribe him with what? The stones we sit on in our final hours?"

His voice raised as if issuing orders. "Outside the western wall, behind the boulder that marks the beggars' grave, is a smaller stone. Under it is a small cavern. He is to leave the map there. If he returns the following night, he will find his payment. We still have friends. His efforts will be well rewarded."

I nodded into the blackness. "That could work."

"It has to."

Through the night, as the snow fell between us, I watched him. He did not move, but I don't believe he slept, either. Twice he tipped his head up as if he could see the stars through the clouds, and sat that way until the snow turned his face white. The hours rolled on until the sky tinged orange.

I had completed the inking and was blowing it dry when the bar grated upwards and the door opened. It was, yet again, the whistler.

Petrov raised his chin and waved the guard closer.

He came.

"I have a task for you," Petrov announced.

I had assumed his tone in outlining the plan to me was only habit. I had assumed he would speak it as a request. I had assumed he would not think to give orders.

I had assumed wrong.

"Behind the beggar's grave is a stone. You are to leave this map under that stone.

The guard stopped. "I am to do *what*?" He spat out the "what" in a fashion I doubted had ever been used to Petrov's face.

Petrov continued unflappably. "If you return the next day, you will find your payment in the form of melin shells. My associates will make it well worth your efforts."

"Melin shells? You think I'd help you for money?"

"It will be enough that you can buy yourself a high seat in the..." his voice quavered for just an instant. Perhaps the guard did not notice, "in the new regime."

"Would it be enough that if I had it now, I could buy the privilege of holding the sword?"

Petrov took a deep breath. "It would be enough, yes."

The guard walked over to where I stood, still holding it flat to dry. He yanked it out of my hands, and I fought down the urge to strike him for his impudence.

"I'll see that your map is taken care of," he muttered, rolling it and undoubtedly smudging the ink before he stalked out.

The door closed and the bar pounded into place before Petrov spoke again.

"He won't do it."

"No," I answered, fighting down guilt at my triumph. "But we had no other choice. There won't be any other guards in here today before…" There was no point in actually saying the words.

Several breaths passed. "We don't have time to make another. We'll have to draw attention to it when we're taken out."

I sighed. It was our last morning. There were better ways to spend it.

"When they take us out," he spoke slowly, formulating the plan as he went, "whether it's together or separate, we will each pick someone at random and tell them the guard has it. Loudly. It will need to be someone at the back of the crowd so we can shout it to them. Tell them which guard has it, and that he took it when we were trying to hide it."

"All right," I muttered. A few hours from my death, it was not worth debating.

The sky remained gray when the door scraped open. Two new guards entered wearing the absurd red armbands the rebels had adopted. "Him first." The short one pointed at Petrov, not even granting him his name or title. "We won't be able to keep the mob under control much longer if we don't give him to them."

Petrov stared back at him, refusing to acknowledge them unless addressed him properly.

"Do we get to drag you out?" The taller one sneered, pulling off his armband in what I can only assume was intended as some sort of inane threat. But in the moment of death, threats lose their power.

Petrov stood slowly, dropping the blanket to the ground with a quiet. "Go with them peacefully when they come for you, Jerov," he said, granting me the dignity of following his orders, not theirs, when my turn came.

I always had the romantic notion that great leaders somehow had profound last words. The final words written in books were always weighty. But in that instant, I realized that final moments are still just moments, and no more likely to be inspired by divine insights than any other moments.

"I will go," I said, "and I'll do as you wish, out of respect for you."

The guards exchanged nervous glances and the taller one yanked him towards the door. The shorter one closed it behind them, staying with me as if they could prevent us from whatever strategy we might be initiating in our last seconds.

His gaze rested on me for a moment, then he turned to run a finger along what was left of a carved ivy leaf above the door.

I finally broke the silence. "Don't you want to watch your king be killed?"

"Why would I want to watch an execution?"

"I thought that's what you all wanted."

He didn't look back at me, just continued to trace the ivy, running his finger in oblong circles again and again. "We want a country where people aren't executed for speaking against the rulers. Your soldiers made me watch when they hung my father for saying we could survive the drought if we had more desalination plants. Why would I want to watch something like that again?"

"We are surviving the drought," I said, pulling my blanket tighter around my shoulders.

"Tell that to the mothers who bury—" His words were cut off by a cheer outside. He didn't repeat himself and I didn't press.

He bent to pick up a piece of the ivy that had fallen, pressing it into the jagged hole in the wall. "Your turn," he said.

I followed his instructions, resting a hand against the wall to brace myself. "The guard who whistles, he has a map to the designs for building more desalination plants," I said. Was I following Petrov's wishes or my own?

He didn't say anything. Maybe he didn't even believe me. He just opened the door and stepped aside when the tall guard grabbed me. Outside, the slush-covered grounds were no less dismal than the roofless palace. A split second later, a roar went up. "Kill him twice," someone shouted, and another yelled, "For my son," just as a brick hit my arm, stabbing pain through my shoulder.

I raised the other arm when the guard shoved me and I fell forward. I lifted my head and searched the crowd for a face I could call Petrov's final instructions to as backup, but another rock hit the back of my head and I couldn't see through the blur of pain. I gasped, throwing up my arms to block when something slammed into my side. I rolled sideways as the blows continued.

I could hear the people cheer, but through the dirty cobbles, all I could see were the stained paper shreds of once-bright fireworks. For a moment, I wished I could cheer with them.

See Dawn Lloyd's story "The Last Duty" online at Metaphorosis.
If you liked it, leave a comment. Authors love that!
Remember to subscribe to our e-mail updates so you'll know when new stories are posted.

About the story

I wrote this story when I was teaching at the American University of Afghanistan. When I first moved to Kabul, I was fortunate that a guard at the bombed out Darul Aman Palace https://en.wikipedia.org/wiki/Darul_Aman_Palace accepted a "tip" to let a group of us inside. I remember one particular guard who followed us around whistling and watching to make sure we didn't go to areas that were so unstable that there was a risk of the roof falling on us. Eventually, the guard's commanding officer came back and told us we weren't allowed to be there. He wasn't inclined to accept a tip to let us stay, either. I lived there for eight years I lived, and every day I looked out my window at the shell of the palace. It was too stark a sight not to ever use in a story.

Sometime around then, when home in the US, I went to the big city 4th of July fireworks. I didn't want to pay to go down close, so I watched them through a chain link fence. Watching the fireworks through a fence led me to wondering what it would feel like for any British loyalists or soldiers to watch the celebrations at the end of the Revolutionary War from less than ideal circumstances. I wasn't sure what I wanted to write, but I knew I had to write something with that theme.

The Darul Aman Palace finally merged with the theme of a fallen ruler watching his people celebrate his demise, and The Last Duty is what came of it.

A question for the author

Q: Are you optimistic about the future of humanity?

A: I am optimistic about the future of humanity because I refuse to be pessimistic. Humanity has overcome everything from the ice age to the black death, not to mention attempted wars, genocides, and a plethora of other things that would be nice to learn how to avoid. None of them have destroyed us entirely, and many of them have made us stronger. I don't know how we'll overcome our current problems, what the next round of problems will be, or what humanity will look like after. I do, however, fully believe that we will survive and continue.

About the author

Dawn Lloyd is an American who got bored and set out across the world looking for adventure. Six countries and four continents later, she teaches at St. Constantine's International School in Tanzania and continues to travel in search of adventure whenever she can.

She is also the Editor in Chief of The Colored Lens (www.thecoloredlens.com)

dawnlloyd.wikispaces.com

The Propagator

Simone Kern

There's a packet of powder taped to my inner thigh, and it feels like the plastic is burning a hole through my leg. Two police officers wave me towards the chem-detecting archway—one last hurdle before I can board the ferry. Sweat pools in the pits of my cooling suit, and my breath comes fast and hot through my respirator. I tell myself they're just city cops, not agents of VerdiCorp. They're just looking for drugs or run-of-the-mill explosives, not the far rarer substance I've stolen. Their arch shouldn't be programmed to catch what I'm carrying.

And it's not.

I pass through without a beep. The cops don't give me a second look. My legs are shaking, but only a small part of that is fear. Lately, whenever I'm near any kind of law enforcement, I see Milo. His tiny body curled on one side, the skin of his face twisted up and back. I see his mouth around the breathing tube, wide with a silent scream, and the gaping hole where the back of his skull should've grown, but didn't.

My blood runs hot with rage. I picture myself pouncing on the bigger cop. Tearing away his air mask. Gouging my fingernails into the soft places of his face.

I am almost getting used to these visions.

I do nothing, of course, but take a steadying breath and force my shaking legs up the gangway. I focus on the feel of the plastic against my thigh. I got away with it. I'm sticking it to the fuckers, in my own way.

Then I'm on board the ferry. A last surge of adrenaline lights up my bloodstream, and suddenly I'm giddy over a crime committed.

The other passengers head inside the purified air of the cabin, eager to shed their bulky outdoor gear. But inside it'll be stuffy and noisy. Every surface—walls, ceiling, seatbacks—will be crowded with the ads I can't bear to see. So I find a spot outside, leaning over the starboard rail. The water slapping the hull is rust-brown, but a strong gulf wind has blown away the usual smog, and the sun gilds each oily wave with a rainbow shimmer.

The ferry pushes away from the docks, carving a path through the labyrinthine chemical refineries towering overhead. The ship channel is choked with rush-hour traffic—gargantuan oil tankers, commuter ferries swapping out day-and-night-shift refinery workers, and the sleek speedboats of executives, darting between us all at breakneck speeds.

We leave the industrial sector behind, smokestacks flaring against the sunset. Winding through sunken neighborhoods, each neon graffiti-scrawled rooftop blazes, like bright flowers sprouting from the murky water. By the time we pass downtown, dusk is falling, and the towers and walkways where the rich live, as high above the waterline as they can afford, glitter against a bruise-colored sky.

High off a close scrape with law enforcement, Houston looks almost beautiful.

Which isn't to say I don't hurt.

I still, always, hurt.

But tonight I'm glad to be watching the stars appear one-by-one in the big Texan sky. I'm glad to see the cube of our habitation block loom up out of the water ahead.

I'm ready to get to work.

Beneath the decontamination showers in the vestibule of our building, I brace myself for the coming onslaught. The hallway and elevator up to our apartment is a gauntlet of triggers. When the last of the polluted water swirls away into the floor, I pull my respirator down and push open the door.

As soon as I step into the hallway, every inch of space—walls, ceiling, floors—bursts to life with ads, designed just for me.

Giggling toddlers wave and run across the walls. They're all the same age Milo would have been.

I unfocus my eyes and hurry forward, trying not to hear. *Time for a toddler-sized stroller? Our air-tight, easy-fold system is lightweight and protects your child from harmful airborne pollutants, like benzene, ozone, metal particulates, and chlorinated hydrocarbons!*

A lot of the ads call my name: *Marisol, buy this! Marisol, you need that!*

But the worst ones are spoken in a toddler's voice:

Mommy, c'n I have a Busy-Bug Indoor Jungle Gym?

Mommy! I want yummy, plant-like snacks from Ponix!

My eyes start to sting. I just have to keep moving. I've tried manually adjusting my ad settings—saying I don't want to see anything with little kids. But every time an ad-scanner catches me out with the stroller, they assume I'm a parent all over again.

The only other ads I get are from VerdiCorp. Every few meters, I get a blessed relief from grinning babies, and the hall is filled with blooming bromeliads and towering *monstera deliciosa* plants instead.

Liven up your living space with VerdiCorp!

Take home a palm, your own slice of paradise. Soil & maintenance included, with no money down, and payments as low as $99.99 a month!

According to the CDC, families with even one plant in the home are 30% less likely to develop cancer. Suicide rates fall for each additional species of plant in a home!

The ad fades as I push the elevator call button, and again I'm surrounded by giggling babies—a toothpaste ad.

As soon as the elevator doors open, I charge in, nearly knocking over our building owner.

"Woah there, Ms. Murphy, what's the hurry?" Rufus chuckles. I slam the doors-closed button. "No little one with you today?"

Like the ad-scanners, he's seen me with the stroller plenty of times, and he's always assumed that beneath the UV-blocking shell, there was a baby inside. I've never felt it wise to correct him.

"Just me," I say, willing the elevator to climb faster.

He leans against the wall and scratches his beard. "Might be some construction going on soon, just a heads-up."

Dread thickens in my stomach. "What's going on?" I try to sound casual.

"Weird thing. Energy bill for the AC keeps going up, even though each apartment's usage is the same. Might be faulty wiring. Thinking about getting an electrician in here to check it out."

My blood's turned to ice. Electricians "checking it out," means poking around in the walls, *behind* the walls, where I'm hiding things far worse than what's in the stolen packet taped to my leg.

"You know Ethan's a journeyman?" I say, in what I hope is a casual tone. "He runs electrical at the plants. I'm sure he could take a look? As a favor?"

"Hey, that'd be great! I like your Ethan. Quiet, but I can tell he's a good guy. Bet he's a good dad too, huh?"

The comment undoes me. Suddenly I'm back in the NICU, watching Ethan hunched over Milo's crib, powerless as me to comfort our dying son.

As soon as the elevator doors open, I mumble a goodbye and bolt for our apartment, past a dozen more squealing toddlers darting across the walls. As soon as I'm inside, I collapse against the door, breathing myself calm in the silence.

The floor of the living area is littered, as always, with the old-timey devices Ethan fixes up for a little extra food money. Analog clocks and desktop computers and mechanical cameras crowd every surface. Ethan sits on the floor in the midst of them, the shape of his back a familiar boulder. He's twisting a screwdriver into the bowels of some dusty, old thing.

"Ethan—Ethan!" I pick my away across the circuit-strewn floor, laying a hand on his shoulder gently. He startles, then pulls one headphone out of his ears.

"Sorry. Just trying to finish this before you got home." He holds up what I now see is a reading light, fitted with a UV bulb. Another grow light for me.

"Thank you," I say, taking the object, although today it sparks more fear than gratitude. "Ethan, I ran into Rufus in the elevator. He's noticed. Says the AC bill keeps going up. He's going to hire an electrician!" My voice is panicked.

"Shit." Ethan rubs a hand down his face.

"I told him you could take a look?" I tug my fingers through my hair. "But maybe we should shut it all down. Dump everything tonight. It's too risky—with this new crop. What the hell was I thinking?"

"No," Ethan cuts me off. He pushes off one knee to stand. Upright, he towers over me. "I'll find Rufus. Tell him it's the smog. It's been affecting power draws over at the plants too. I'll offer to pressure-wash the solar roof. That should help with his bill."

"Are you sure?" I ask, "I mean—about all of it?"

Our eyes meet, and it's a shock. How long has it been since we last held each other's gaze? His eyes seem to have gotten paler—filtered-water-blue.

"I'm sure," he says, pulling me close. He speaks again into my hair, his voice more loving, more decisive than I've heard in a long time.

"Grow your flowers, Marcy."

I used to be terrified of breaking the law, afraid I might do it by accident. When I was eight years old, my school gave us this "Kid's Guide to Texas Law" trivia hologame that I obsessively re-played, memorizing every right answer. As I got older, learned how the world worked—how badly the odds were stacked against folks from habitation blocks like mine—I only became more determined to avoid arrest.

But after Milo, nothing seemed to matter anymore.

Ironically, it was a trip to a prison that sparked my criminal career. It was my first day back at VerdiCorp from bereavement leave, and I was still so sick with grief that I didn't really pay attention to the details when my shift manager explained the job at Sugarland Correctional. I just punched in the order and let the warehouse drones load my boat to capacity, only vaguely registering how massive the order was—20 cubic yards of D-Grade soil, 2000 square feet of Bermuda sod. Grief had robbed me of curiosity. There was only getting through the hours of the work day, earning enough pay so I could bring home something to eat with Ethan. Why I kept going through the motions of this life, and whether I should keep doing it, were questions I couldn't answer.

At the prison docks, my fleet of drones started unloading the cargo and a mustached guard told me I'd be installing a new green space in Cell Block D—Reproductive Crimes.

It was like a sick joke. I'd let Milo suffer to avoid being sent to this place. Now guilt socked me in the gut, solid as a fist, and I struggled to breathe as the guard led me through a series of chem scanners and locked steel doors. My installation drones trundled behind us, hauling the massive bio-storage drums and rolls of sod.

As soon as we passed through the gates of Cell Block D, hundreds of furious eyes from three stories of cells fell upon us, and a howling started up, like the first gusts of a hurricane. The inmates were cursing and wailing, kicking the bars and their beds. Many of them were pregnant—women and trans men. I saw one guy, scraggly beard and swollen belly, must've been nine months along. He was chained to his bed, sobbing into his hands.

The guard leaned towards me, and for a moment I thought he was going to arrest me. Like he also knew what was in my rotten heart. But slowly, I processed what he was shouting over the din. "They thought their little 'protest' would get them something better than that," he pointed back at my drones and their rolls of sod.

We stepped through another set of doors into a blessedly quiet corridor, and his voice dropped to a normal volume. "We meet all the legal requirements. Every inmate gets an hour a day of green time, and we have 1 square foot of lawn for every girl. But that wasn't good enough for them."

We reached a set of steel doors. Above them a sign read: *The Garden.*

"They went on hunger strike. Even the pregnant ones. Wrote up a list of demands —there were like twenty different species of plants on it!" He snorted, swiping his hand over a DNA-reader.

The doors slid open, and we stepped into what used to be a gymnasium— rusting basketball hoops still clung to the walls. But the center of the tile floor had been dug out and replaced with grass— mostly dead now. Huge swaths of brown criss-crossed a few remaining patches of green lawn.

"The warden ordered the medical staff to force-feed the girls. They lost their damn minds over that," he shook his head. "There was a riot, and some of them did this. Got into the cleaning stores and poured bleach all over the grass. I guess they thought we'd replace it with something better," he snorted. "If you ask me, they should lose their green time altogether for this, but the warden says that'll get us into legal trouble. Damn ACLU."

I said nothing, wanting to just finish the job and get the hell out of there. I was still shaken by the inmates' screams. I didn't want to know their stories. I didn't have room in my heart for anyone else's pain.

"Someone needs to sign for the product," I said, passing him my tablet.

"What is this?"

"Terms of your lease," I rattled through the spiel robotically. "VerdiCorp reserves all rights to the living matter. Propagation of plants without a permit is a violation of federal law. Soil is to be used only for growing plants leased through VerdiCorp, and any maintenance, fertilization, or pest control must be contracted through VerdiCorp."

The guard scrawled his signature, then left me alone in the cavernous space. Most of the soil was unsalvageable—poisoned by the dioxin in the bleach. But in the corners of the lawn, the grass was still green. I sent my drones to start digging out all the contaminated soil and called my manager. I asked her what to do about the soil that was still okay.

"All the soil is to be replaced."

"A lot of it is still good."

"They ordered all-new soil, so give them all-new soil."

"I bet there's a cubic yard or more of healthy dirt—"

"Marisol? It's a government contract. All the soil is to be replaced," her tone deepened, barring any future discussion.

"Okay. Got it," I said, hanging up. But I just stared at the pit. The good soil there could provide green space for a hundred families. I couldn't bring myself to order the drones to pack it in with the dioxin-poisoned earth.

I started picturing what could've been done with this space, and with the amount of money the prison had spent on the order. Instead of 2,000 square feet of monotonous lawn, they could've had a slightly smaller tropical garden, complete with trees and vines and flowering plants, and they still would've fallen well within the legal requirements for green space. Was it laziness or cruelty that made the warden order 2,000 square feet of the same damn plant, when he could've just as easily ordered the twenty different species the inmates wanted?

Or maybe he thought he had to punish them for the protest. To control them.

Imprisoned and shackled to their beds. Force-fed and forced to watch their bellies swell. Was it too much to ask that they get to look at some fucking flowers?

And suddenly I understood exactly why they'd poured bleach all over their "garden." Blood pounded hot in my ears, my muscles started to shake, and I felt it too, then. Blood-on-fire, fuck-the-consequences, burn-the-world-down rage.

I wanted to wail like the inmates and kick my drones to pieces. I wanted to find that asshole warden and drive my fingers through the skin of his neck. The clarity and specificity of that vision scared me, but it was also exhilarating. I hadn't felt anything but numbing grief since Milo's death. At least the desire for violence was a *desire*.

But surely I was under surveillance. I couldn't make any sudden movements, let alone enact destruction. I forced myself to take some deep breaths. And as I watched my drones dig, I realized there was something I could do that would be a fuck-you to Sugarland Correctional, and VerdiCorp, and my bitch of a manager, and even that asshole warden.

I could save the good soil.

Fingers shaking, I programmed my drones to gather up the healthy soil in a separate 200-gallon storage drum from the contaminated earth. My mind raced. What the hell would I do with it? I was supposed head straight from here to WasteWerks, to turn over all the drums of earth. If I showed up back at the warehouse with one drum remaining, my manager would probably fire me just for subverting her authority. I certainly couldn't bring a whole drum of dirt home. I'd have to stash it somewhere.

The soil was the property of VerdiCorp, and even though they didn't want it, were just going to give it to WasteWerks to shore up a barrier island outside the city, that wouldn't matter in a court of law. While in transit, the soil belonged to my employers, and stashing it somewhere was theft.

I was angry enough not to care. I couldn't give these inmates the garden they deserved, but I could steal this soil. I could use it to make things grow.

On the way back to the warehouse, I ran my boat up alongside the third story of a brick mansion in a sunken neighborhood. I had a drone maneuver the drum through a window, shattered long ago. Then I rigged a power surge to flood my drones' charging stations, forcing a reboot that wiped their memories of the entire job. As my boat puttered away through rotting tree-tops, part of me hoped an anarchist gang would find the drum before I returned. I knew already that stolen soil would lead me towards greater crimes, though I couldn't see the shape of them just yet.

When I got home, I told Ethan what I'd done. That I wanted to use the stolen soil to propagate VerdiCorp plants—a federal crime. I'd be putting us both at risk. Was he okay with that?

He looked up from a disemboweled stereo system long enough to shrug and say he didn't care. It was the most we'd talked in days, both of us lost in a grief that made everything seem pointless.

That night I couldn't sleep, and not for the usual reasons. I wandered the apartment, looking for something I could use to transport the soil. The mop-bucket was a good size but didn't have a lid. I needed something airtight, so the soil wouldn't get contaminated by airborne toxins in transit. The Tupperware in the kitchen was too small—transporting the soil that way would take years. Finally, in the back of my closet, I found the perfect thing.

UV-blocking, self-contained air filtration, and it held about a gallon of dirt. It was the fancy stroller Ethan's mom had given us, before we knew. I hadn't had the heart to sell it yet.

So I ventured out just after midnight, loading the stroller into Ethan's dinghy. I was worried I wouldn't be able to find the right house in the darkness, but after puttering around the sunken River Oaks neighborhood, my searchlight fell on a familiar stretch of brick. Inside, I found the drum of soil, untouched. I quickly shoveled a few armfuls of dirt into the stroller, then sealed its beetle-shell lid against the toxic air.

At that time, Ethan and I only had one plant—a neon-green pothos we'd been leasing for years. Its vines wrapped around the walls of the living room, dangling from hooks we'd drilled as supports. That night, I snipped a handful of pothos leaves, just past where they met the vine, and dropped them in water. A few days later, the pothos cuttings had sprouted roots, and I transferred each one to a Tupperware of stolen soil.

From one living thing, many. A theft of VerdiCorp's profits.

Each night for the weeks that followed, I repeated my midnight trip to the sunken neighborhood, hauling about a gallon of soil a night. We started saving food containers for use as growing pots. Ethan scoured the junkyards for light fixtures to turn into grow lamps. Pothos cuttings took over every surface of the kitchen. I loved that profusion of neon green, but if someone were to go in there—Rufus, maybe, snooping while we were at work—it would be obvious we were running a criminal growing operation.

The electric bill had shot up from all the grow lights running 24/7, and our water usage had nearly doubled. One night Ethan asked if I had any plans for what to do with all our new plants, or was I just trying to get us arrested? A fair question, and I didn't have an answer.

The next day, I had off work, and I headed to the city botanical gardens, pushing the stroller, a small razor tucked up in my sleeve. I wanted to see if I could sneak cuttings of some other species of plants.

Beneath the cavernous glass dome of the tropical gardens, the shrieks of countless kids running up and down the paths grated on my ears. The gardens were always jam-packed on Saturdays with families that couldn't afford their own gardens. I was bent over a fire-colored croton plant, trying to work up the courage to sneakily slice off a leaf, when a small body barreled into me, knocking me into the croton.

I slipped a few crushed leaves up my sleeve as I straightened up. A parent rushed over to me, brushing off their kid. "Sorry, sorry! He shouldn't have been running." Both of them had golden-brown skin and long, loose curls.

"No trouble," I said, glad for the chance to sneak a few cuttings. "I think the plant is okay."

"They're so easy when they're little, aren't they?"

"Really? I think they're more finicky. Can't afford to dry out at all, roots aren't established."

She looked at me quizzically, and it took us both a second.

"Oh, you meant...?" I gestured to the stroller.

"Yea. Kids. When they're little, you can just set them down anywhere."

"I was talking about plants."

"I got that," she laughed warmly. There was something about her I instantly liked.

A genuineness. Her name was Danni, a teacher.

"Do you have any? Plants?" I asked, gesturing to the croton.

"No, no. We've been saving up for an ivy or something, but with five kids…" she trailed off. "Anyways, that's why we come here so often."

The thought of five kids growing up without a single stem of green at home made me come to a rash decision. My next words would make me something worse than a thief or a propagator in the eyes of the law. I'd be a dealer, subject to minimum sentencing laws of ten years federal prison.

The din of happy children's screams was probably loud enough to obscure my voice from ad scanners, but I whispered anyways.

"You want one?"

A few days after I met Danni, the shower ran cold again, and rather than risk inviting Rufus into the apartment, Ethan decided to fix the plumbing himself. While shining his flashlight back among the pipes, he discovered that above the building's air- and water-recycling ducts, a secret crawlspace ran the length of the building. It was an answer to many of our problems.

Tonight, I take the new grow light Ethan made me into the bathroom and remove the plumbing access panel behind the shower. I squeeze through the narrow opening between the hot water pipe and the wall and push through a curtain of purple-and-green *trandescantia pallida* leaves, emerging into my garden.

The ceiling is only five feet high, so I stoop as I make my way towards the cluttered desk where I do my propagating. Shelves line the walls, loaded with dozens of species of plants, all blazing in the light of a hundred mismatched grow lights. Ethan rigged it so all of them are plugged directly into the power line for the building's AC. We don't pay the bills, Rufus does, and now he's noticed the increase.

After I gave her that first pothos, I told Danni to tell her friends about me. Word spread that there was a lone woman with a black stroller who hung out in the botanical gardens on weekends, who would give some green to any plantless parents. I delivered the plants to their homes directly, tucked inside the stroller. A few times I ran into police checkpoints, but they never asked me to open the UV shield—an absurd bit of luck.

In the homes of my clients, I accepted their luke-warm mugs of Koffee and instructed them in proper plant care. I told them to hide the plants away in a back room, to avoid the suspicion of neighbors. Every time I knocked on a client's door, my heart was in my throat— never knowing whether I'd been set up, whether agents from VerdiCorp were waiting inside with handcuffs.

And then one afternoon, sitting on a bench in the botanical garden, someone approached me who didn't seem to be a parent. No kids in tow. Nose ring, stripe-shaved head, anarchist tattoos crawling up their tanned arms, and spider legs drawn around their sharp-cornered eyes. I had never been approached by a non-parent before. Would I give to one? Was it worth the risk? I was doing this for the kids, right? If I gave to one anarchist punk, how many more would come—

"Marisol?" They sat right next to me.

My heartrate spiked. Besides Danni, I'd been careful never to tell clients my name. "I'm sorry. Do I know you?"

"We have a mutual friend." They raised their eyebrows meaningfully. "Lilith?"

A friend of Lilith's...a friend of Lilith's...the phrase stuck in my mind, like a half-remembered nursery rhyme. It meant something—something high school kids giggled about. Anarchist slang, maybe. I couldn't remember.

"I'm sorry, you have the wrong person," I said, moving to stand.

Their hand clamped over my wrist, their voice urgent. "Lilith knows about Milo. What you *had* to do."

I sank back down, fighting to keep my face impassive.

"Lilith helps people who are...like you were."

Suddenly it clicks. Friend of Lilith. "She's gone to see a friend of Lilith." That's what kids would say when someone met a doctor at a sunken home, late at night, maybe never to emerge. "She tried to visit Lilith." That meant one of our classmates was in the hospital for eating a box of laxatives. Or digging inside themselves with an unbent coat hanger.

They waited for a clump of screaming kids to run by to whisper, "We know you're a grower, and we have something that needs growing. You can help Lilith in her work."

They pressed a twist of paper into my palm and stood abruptly. "We'll be in touch."

I was supposed to feel horrified. I was supposed to flag down the nearest police officer and report them. But I didn't. And by the time I thought to ask, "How do you know I'll help you?" they had already disappeared down the crowded path towards the desert biome.

I peeled back one corner of the paper and peeked. Inside were half-a-dozen tiny, black seeds.

At first, I thought the ultrasound tech was just unfriendly. She slathered cold jelly on my belly, her face set in a grim line. I wanted to chat about names and nesting, but she was all business, pushing the wand vigorously into my flesh. Now, of course, I understand her reserve. With each passing year, she must see more and more pregnancies like mine. To a parent, even a smile from her might seem like a promise she can't keep. The only words I remember her saying were, "I'm going to get the doctor."

Dr. Lavan's eyes were kind and stayed glued to mine when he told us that our baby had a neural tube defect. "A worst-case scenario."

I made him repeat the ugly word, write it down for me, until my tongue could wrap around it, as if that would give me some control: craniorachischisis.

Our baby's neural tube had never closed, would never close, and so both his brain and spinal cord were exposed to the amniotic fluid. No baby born with craniorachischisis had ever survived longer than two days outside the womb.

Dr. Lavan warned me against searching the term on the net. The pictures would be disturbing, he said.

Ethan's hands clamped like vices on my shoulders. I was nearly shouting at Dr. Lavan then, like my protests could change anything. "But I took my prenatals! I've always worn my respirator! Hell, I've tried not to go outside at all!"

"This is just something that happens," he said, so kindly. "It could be genetic. Or you could have been exposed to something years ago. There's nothing to be gained by placing blame."

I could barely get out the next words. "Is he in pain?"

Dr. Lavan paused for too long. "I don't know."

I broke down crying then, knowing it was a lie.

"I've worked with parents in your situation before. This will be hard—for both of you." He turned to Ethan. "I'm going to write you each a prescription for mood stabilizers—"

"Oh, so your ass is covered?" I snapped. "If I lose my mind over the next five months and throw myself—" The warning look on Dr. Lavan's face stopped me, reminded me that every word we said was being recorded, subject to review by life enforcement detectives.

He spoke very slowly. "Given the nature of this pregnancy, it's very important that we do everything possible to maximize your baby's chance of survival. You'll need to be diligent in taking your vitamins, no risky food choices, and be sure not to miss a single check-up."

He didn't need to say the "or else." I knew—if this baby died before birth, we'd both be investigated for evidence of wrongdoing.

He risked his medical license with the next sentence, lingering on two words, letting me know how carefully they were chosen. "I am not a neural tube specialist, but if you were able to...travel...to see a specialist, they might have more... options...for you."

He meant that if we could get North, make it to Illinois, or West to California, there were doctors there who could end the pregnancy.

In that moment, I was furious with him. I had been taught from elementary school to look with horror on the years before *Turner vs. Alabama.* To feel superior to all those lawless, Northern states where the genocide of the unborn continued unabated. And Dr. Lavan knew how badly we wanted this baby. How we'd been trying to conceive for more than a year. I had cried, sitting on the toilet, over a dozen negative pregnancy tests, and I had cried for joy when I'd finally gotten to tell him our good news.

But as soon as we got home from the ultrasound, of course I immediately searched the internet for "chranioarachischisis." I saw the pictures of those tiny, blue-skinned bodies with their gaping skulls, and I knew the shape of agony growing inside me.

And so late that night, holding each other in bed, Ethan and I discussed it. If there was no conceivable way our baby could live, if he was in pain, then maybe Dr. Lavan was right. Maybe we should see a "specialist." But there was no way we could afford the trip across three states, let alone the thousands the procedure would cost. It would be cheaper and closer to get to Mexico, but crossing the border could be deadly. And even if we did somehow raise the money, once it was done, we could never return home, or we'd be arrested the moment we crossed into Texas.

I needed a "friend of Lilith" then, but I didn't know how to find one. I knew there were ways to do it yourself, but I was more likely to kill myself trying. Even searching the internet for answers could get me arrested. And if I wound up at the hospital for any reason, even just food poisoning, I'd face investigation for repro crimes.

So we did nothing. I waited for the long months of my pregnancy to tick by. My symptoms worsened—nausea and cramps and heartburn, aching breasts and back and feet. I was in pain and exhausted all the time. It must feel different, for parents of healthy babies. For me, each day I was pregnant was more miserable than the last. When I couldn't think of a reason to get out of bed anymore, I started taking Dr. Lavan's mood stabilizers.

The baby grew. I tried not to think of him as my son. I tried not to think of him at all. But like any healthy baby, he became impossible to ignore as the months dragged by. I felt his first hiccups, and then his first kicks, but there was no joy in those flutters. I guessed that with each movement, he was writhing in pain.

Sometimes I wanted to claw him out with my fingernails.

Sometimes I wanted to lean over the rail of the ferry and sink to the flooded streets below.

And sometimes, late at night, my lifelong disbelief didn't seem to matter, and I'd curl around my swollen stomach, praying for a miracle. For his skull to grow, for the skin along the back of his spine to knit shut, his face relaxing into a smile.

More often, though, I prayed for him to die. In a spontaneous, painless, medically conclusive way that would absolve me of any wrongdoing.

He didn't, so at 39 weeks, Dr. Lavan was legally obligated to remove him from my body via C-Section, as the baby would have a greater likelihood of surviving that operation than a vaginal birth. Dr. Lavan didn't have a choice in the matter, and neither, of course, did I. The law guided his hand, as he sliced through the flesh of my belly, then my uterus, extricated my mangled child, and reassembled me.

Milo Lopez McMannis (they forced us to name him) lived for forty-three hours after his birth. Nearly a world record. I wasn't allowed to hold him while he was still alive. After, the nurse offered me his corpse, wrapped in a blanket, but I said no. I think Ethan did hold him. I don't remember much, honestly. Dr. Lavan had given me a blessedly strong cocktail of painkillers that let me sleep through most of Milo's life and the days that followed.

Dr. Lavan said we could try again if we liked. That there was a good chance my next baby would be normal. But just in case, I wasn't going to let Ethan so much as kiss my neck after that. He never tried.

I had done what they wanted. I'd been a good girl. I'd thought that if I stayed on the right side of the law, when it was all over, my life would to go back to normal. But I couldn't turn back into the girl I was before I grew a dying boy, any more than I could erase that mocking scar slashed across my belly.

Two weeks after Milo's death, I was back at work. And I found myself standing in a cell block for reproductive criminals, staring at a mostly-dead lawn.

It took twenty-three days for the mystery seeds to germinate. Of the six, four sprouted into seedlings, and the next time I visited the botanical gardens, Lilith's friend was waiting at my usual bench.

"Seen any interesting plants today?" they asked quietly as I sat down.

"Some kind of plumbago, but I don't know the species. There's no record of it in the database at work."

"I wouldn't go searching the net to find it. You might trip an algorithm."

My guess was correct, then. This particular plumbago must be an abortifacient.

"You expect me to work for you, but I've been thinking. This plant—it couldn't have helped me, right? I was too far along by the time I knew I needed it?"

"Probably," they said. "But your friend Danni? She's the one who told us about you. She needed us a few weeks ago, and we were able to help, because of other growers like you."

I thought of Danni and her husband, five kids already, all of them crammed into an apartment smaller than me and Ethan's. I didn't know how she fed them all as it was.

"I do want to help," I said slowly. "But someone who takes this…they could end up getting sick, right? Even dying?"

"There are no guarantees." They pursed their lips. "But Lilith has many friends. Chemists, doctors, midwives …going through us is much safer than going it alone."

"Is it in the flowers?"

"The root."

I let out a rush of air. "That'll take time." It'd be another month or two for this batch to flower, another few weeks to produce seeds. At that point I could start a new crop and harvest the four measly roots I'd grown, but who knew if I'd still be a free citizen by then?

Of course, if I could propagate the plumbago from cuttings, rather than seeds—that would greatly speed up my growing times. But plumbago species were tricky to propagate. I would need rooting hormone—a Class A controlled substance. There was plenty of it in the vault at VerdiCorp.

I just had to steal some without getting caught.

The plumbago has just started to blossom, filling the crawlspace with heady perfume. Reaching into my pants, I peel the packet of stolen rooting hormone off my thigh. I grasp a clump of bright white blossoms.

With a sharp scissors, I cut off a leaf cluster just below the node and dip the severed stem in the packet of rooting hormone. I drop the stem in a cup of water, then choose another clump of leaves to amputate.

When I finish, I have twenty new plants. If the roots take, they'll grow much faster than those I started from seed.

Soon, all the pothos, monstera, and kalanchoe I've lovingly cultivated will have to be composted to make room for more plumbago. It'd be too risky to try and distribute so many plants so quickly, and I mean to grow as much as I possibly can.

Lilith's friend said one six-inch root can make four doses. I stare around the crawlspace and do the math, imagining the shelves loaded with white blossoms floor-to-ceiling. My only fear is that I won't stay free long enough to see it. An electrician could bust through the wall and discover my garden. The neighbors might notice the sweet floral smell. Maybe I already got caught on camera, earlier today, slipping that packet of rooting hormone up my sleeve. Or maybe "Lilith's friend" is really a life-enforcement detective, and this whole thing has been a setup.

However it comes, I sense in my bones that time is running out. You can't grow a garden like this in Texas and get away with it forever. Ethan knows it too.

But he said, "Grow your flowers, Marcy."

When I'm caught, I'll be lucky to get life in prison. But fear isn't what keeps me awake each night. It's the wanting to go back in time, to the day I got the diagnosis. I should've chugged a fifth of vodka, hung around crowded places, asking for "Lilith." I should have followed Dr. Lavan home and demanded he give me "options." I should have shown a shred of courage. Tried *something* to end Milo's suffering.

Because the moment I saw him, I knew.

All he did was suffer.

I like to think that when they come for me with handcuffs, I'll hold my head high. That I'll wear a smile when they lead me into the courtroom, strap me to a table for the last breaths of my life.

The world will know, then. I was one of Lilith's friends.

*See Simone Kern's story "The Propagator"
online at Metaphorosis.
If you liked it, leave a comment. Authors love
that!
Remember to subscribe to our e-mail updates so
you'll know when new stories are posted.*

About the story

I live near the Houston ship channel, the chemical refinery capital of America, so both the causes and effects of climate change are right at our doorstep.

Summers are brutally hot, and the city (and our house) floods regularly. In March of 2019 we had a major industrial accident, the ITC plant fire, which put a black cloud of poisonous smoke right over our house. The setting of this story came to me shortly afterwards, from thinking about what the Gulf Coast might look like 50-75 years on, if nothing is done to curtail climate change or the deregulation of the oil & gas industry.

In that flooded, toxic, boiling-hot world, green spaces will be at a premium, and left unchecked, corporations will surely exploit the fundamental human need for green space. Already, Monsanto has developed such a stranglehold over agriculture that seed-saving is now illegal. Given enough profit potential, I imagine corporations will seek to exert the same level of control over every type of plant.

I knew I wanted a character who defied these laws by propagating houseplants, but I didn't get her motivation until I heard about Texas HB1500--a heartbeat abortion ban that was up before the Texas legislature. This bill ultimately failed, but similar bans passed in Alabama, Georgia, and now Missouri. I saw a connection there—between forced birth and patented plants. Who controls biological reproduction? Increasingly, we see that power moving away from individuals towards more powerful entities.

For people who've never experienced it (including most lawmakers passing these bills), pregnancy is an abstraction. We too often speak about pregnancy in euphemisms, when it is a wall-to-wall traumatic experience that forever changes you, even when the fetus is healthy & wanted. I wanted readers to confront what it would mean to be forced to carry a pregnancy to term against your will, against all common sense. I wanted them to understand how that would alter you forever, as it does Marisol. I've not been in Marisol's situation, but I have my own share of reproductive traumas. So I drew on some of my own fear and rage and grief from those experiences, and I hope I did her story justice.

Finally, Milo's condition stems from the correlation between air pollution and severe fetal abnormalities. I'm a parent, living in the shadow of chemical refineries, who checks the local news before we play outside in case there's been a benzene leak that day. The same politicians who support forced birth also fight against any effort to curtail air pollution. Marisol's situation encapsulates the absurd and horrifying conclusion of their policy platform.

A question for the author

Q: What's the story no one else thinks is as good as you do?

A: *Twin Study* by Stacey Richter is a whole book of short stories that was critically well-received but never became the best-seller it deserved to be. This is the kind of book you shouldn't read on an airplane, because you'll creep out everyone around you by alternately gasping and crying and laughing out loud.

I'm still haunted by sentences from this book that are so good, they'll give me imposter syndrome forever.

In college, my fiction professor, Dan Chaon, was a big fan of Richter's, and that's how I came across *Twin Studies*. At the time, Richter maintained a Q&A on her website, and my roommate and I, both aspiring 19-year-old writers obsessed with *Twin Study*, would frequently come home late at night and send her drunken questions about writing or dating, which she always answered with pithy brilliance. A decade later, I was teaching English IV to a class suffering from a particularly bad case of senioritis and, after failing to interest them in Hemingway and *Hamlet*, assigned some stories out of *Twin Study*. Kids who hadn't done the reading all year were busting with opinions on "The Cavemen in the Hedges", and probably the single most important class discussion of my teaching career came from talking about date rape after reading the story "Blackout". Every story in *Twin Study* is a treasure, and Richter should rank alongside Kelly Link, Karen Russell, and A. M. Homes as one of the best living short story writers. Go read it and thank me later!

About the author

Simone Kern grew up in a small town in Illinois, where they were definitely the only Jewish-atheist-socialist-genderqueer kid in school. After studying creative writing at Oberlin College, they moved to Houston where they taught English in public schools for ten years. After the birth of their kid, Simone quit teaching to write and be a stay-at-home parent. They love-hate Houston, because their house floods, and it's too hot, and nearby chemical refineries keep exploding, but the people are just too good to leave. Thus, Simone has embraced life as a bayou creature and is busy learning the names of all the Texas wildflowers.

www.simonekernwrites.com, @simone__kern

There is a City, He Told Me

Evan James Sheldon

There is a city where the outer walls shift and entrances dance away, so that a passerby might think they are merely approaching from the wrong side. If you know about this city, if you are patient and cunning, you can find a way in, and what a city! Its interior is not flashy, not filled with magicians and trees burning with inner fire, but there is comfort there you can find with diligence and pursuit. People leave, as they will, and the inhabitants wait longingly for those travelers to return, for the simple joy of conversing with someone else who understands the city's intricacies.

I can see my father forming the words, and it is not yet a struggle. His patchy steel-wool beard parts right before he says each phrase, like his own body knows what he is going to say. I haven't heard of these cities in years and they've changed during my time away, they are different cities now. Maybe his purpose is less veiled. Maybe my understanding of what he speaks, his intent, has deepened, but either way tonight, I understand his meaning.

His hands shake. But his voice does not waver. It is strong, mellifluous, golden, and sweetened by the red-and-white-striped peppermint candies that clack against his teeth as he speaks, providing a counterpoint rhythm to his cadence. I had forgotten about the candy.

There is a city where the young people paint their teeth black so that it looks as if they have no teeth at all. They guffaw and toss bits of food at the elderly, taunting and smacking their lips. This practice continued until one child painted their teeth gold. Now they turn their faces, their mockery, to the sun. The very old lounge in the shade of tall trees while the faces of the young burn to a crisp, tongues wagging.

His words come slower, still clear but plodding. I pull the blanket up and tuck it beneath his beard. It is the same color, a rough steely wool, and it looks as if his beard extends to the floor, pooling there. I wonder how long he has sat in the chair by the fire, waiting for me. I wonder if he can see the darkening of foreign suns on my cheeks and forehead.

There is a city that moves, that picks up shop and will relocate to a new place on a whim. The inhabitants believe it is not the city that has moved, but the rest of the world. That the earth beneath their feet has shifted through no fault of their own. They come to believe in a conspiracy of geography and leave markers, carvings to indicate locations they know.

He believes that these places are real. You can tell by the tenor in his voice, his fervor, the way his cloudy eyes remain on my face. He knows these places. He thinks about the inhabitants. That girl who ran across the muddy lane wearing only one shoe. That couple who drifted in and out of traffic, oblivious to the sirens, to the honk and bustle of the city. That woman who painted her body to match the sky and stood frozen in the square, reduced to an outline, a shimmering against the clouds.

Maybe they are real, conjured by his retelling. Maybe they have always been real, and I have just been searching when I should have been understanding.

There is a city where the ghosts never leave. They stay. They linger. The city's inhabitants push through transparent faces and fingers like a permanent fog. The living have become used to the lingering ghosts, and paint their houses with bright, vibrant colors to find their way. The living paint their faces in elaborate designs to see one another smile. The living laugh and move through life unencumbered by those that have come before them. In the ghost's desire to stay, they have in fact, become invisible.

When he stops speaking I hold up my hand to his mouth. There is warmth there and breath still. He is afraid, but even now, he will only speak of cities. What can I say to assure him that I won't forget? I form the words, but they feel flat, inadequate on my tongue. I stoke the fire and wait.

There is a city made and sustained only by songs sung by children and no one is ever left alone in silence.

There was a time when I would not have waited. There was a time when I was off visiting my own cities, searching to see if what he said was true. I wonder now whom he told of these places in my absence, or if they bottled inside of him, waiting for me and only me, to spill out when I returned.

There is a city where they only decorate in bleached bones of their fathers, a celebration, a homage.

Or if he has been speaking slowly, continually, trying to call me back.

There is a city where rain bursts from the ground and all the trees twist roots into the sky, where a person might walk right into the heavens.

There is a city that everyone visits, but never returns from.

There is a city...

There is a city...

There is a city...

This time when he stops, I know he is done. I hold my hand to his mouth and there is no movement. He is finally quiet. I linger for a moment, in the firelight his beard and his blanket shine like hammered metal.

When I get home, my daughter rushes into my arms. I am grateful for the rain to hide my tears, but she is too smart, too quick. But she doesn't say anything when she lays her head on my chest. We sit by the fire and listen to it crackle. *Did you know, little one, that there is a city where an old man grew a metal beard? He always sat by a fire that never dies. And the words he spoke were false, but he never lied. And when his time came, his son wrapped him up tight in the metal that grew from his face so he would be warm for his journey. Because he could no longer stay.*

Why couldn't he stay? she asks.

Because he had new cities to see, a hundred hundred new places to visit.

She is quiet, but her eyes grow wide, and in the light of my own fire, they shine like living ore.

See Evan James Sheldon's story "There is a City, He Told Me" online at Metaphorosis.
If you liked it, leave a comment. Authors love that!
Remember to subscribe to our e-mail updates so you'll know when new stories are posted.

About the story

I wrote, "There is a City, He told me," after reading Calvino's *Invisible Cities*. In that short novel, Marco Polo describes the Kahn's empire to him through a series of flash-length sections. Reading, you come to realize that Marco Polo is actually talking about something else, and in the end (Spoilers!) a descent into hell. Instead of making a broad philosophical statement, I wanted to show how this form could function on a smaller, relational level. When I was writing this my wife and I were expecting our first child, a girl, and it seemed like a natural fit.

A question for the author

Q: Do you often include children in your stories? What role do they play?

A: I do often write about children, though I find I normally write from their perspective. I love to use some of the formal elements found in fairy tales in my stories, and even in darker stories, children offer decisive action and reaction that is, I hope, relatable for the reader. In this story, the daughter at the end provides a way for the mythmaking narrative to make sense and provides insight into the narrator's understanding of his relationship with his father. My wife and I are expecting our first child, a daughter, any day, and thinking about the stories that we will tell her helped to shape the emotional arc in this story.

About the author

Evan James Sheldon is a Senior Editor for F(r)iction and the Editorial Coordinator for Brink Literacy Project. He lives in Denver with his wife and soon-to-arrive daughter.

evanjamessheldon.com, @EvanJamesSheld1

Copyright

Metaphorosis Publishing

Metaphorosis offers beautifully written science fiction and fantasy. Our projects include:

Metaphorosis Magazine

Metaphorosis, a weekly magazine of SFF short stories, including stories from all the authors in this anthology. Find out more at magazine.metaphorosis.com, and sign up to be notified of new stories.

Metaphorosis Books

Recent books from Metaphorosis can be found at <u>books.metaphorosis.com</u>, and include:

Score

an SFF symphony

What if stories were written like music? *Score* is an anthology of stories written to an emotional score.

Best Vegan SFF of 2018

The best vegan science fiction and fantasy stories of 2018!

Metaphorosis 2018

All the stories from *Metaphorosis* magazine's third year. Fifty-two great SFF stories.

Metaphorosis: Best of 2018

The best science fiction and fantasy stories from *Metaphorosis* magazine's third year.

Metaphorosis 2017

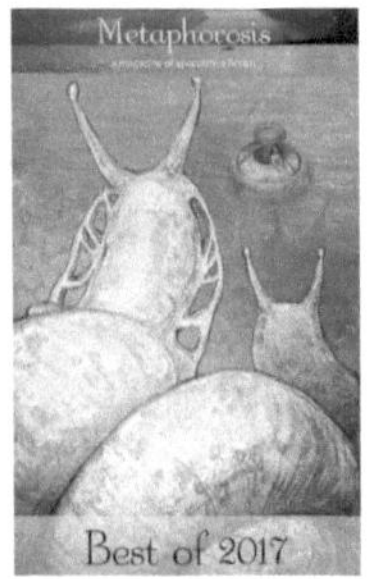

Metaphorosis: Best of 2017

All the stories from *Metaphorosis* magazine's second year. Fifty-three great SFF stories.

The best science fiction and fantasy stories from *Metaphorosis* magazine's *second* year.

Metaphorosis
2016

Almost all the stories from *Metaphorosis* magazine's first year.

Metaphorosis:
Best of 2016

The best science fiction and fantasy stories from *Metaphorosis* magazine's first year.

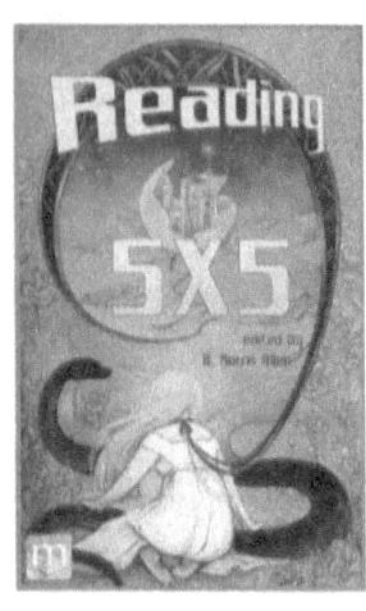 

Reading 5X5	**Reading 5X5**

Five stories, five times

Twenty-five SFF authors, five base stories, five versions of each – see how different writers take on the same material, with stories in contemporary and high fantasy, soft and hard SF, and a mysterious 'other' category.

Writers' Edition

All the stories from the regular, readers' edition, plus two extra stories, the story seed, and authors' notes on writing. Over 100 pages of additional material specifically aimed at writers.

Best Vegan SFF of 2017

The best vegan science fiction and fantasy stories of 2017!

Best Vegan SFF of 2016

The best vegan science fiction and fantasy stories of 2016!

Susurrus

A darkly romantic story of magic, love, and suffering.

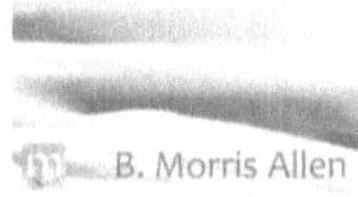